The Adventures of

A New Beginning

Written by: Marty Hartman

Illustrated by: Andrew Chandler

The Adventures of Wally the Wheelchair: A New Beginning

First ed., October, 2010. Edited by Connie Chandler

ISBN-13:978-1466259683

Dedicated to the memory of Lonnie Oliver Hartman,

my grandfather,

who bought me my very first wheelchair at the age of three.

To
Malachi,
I hope you enjoy
the book! Remember to
always dream big and let
God take care of the rest!

Your friend,
Marty Walker

Luke 1:37

The day begun just like any other day since he had arrived

at Matthews' Medicine Shoppe in the small town of

Midasville.

He sat in the window as the people walked by,

and his mind wandered back to the day it all started...

He remembered being nothing more than a few metal rods, a couple of pieces of fabric, four wheels and a bunch of nuts and bolts.

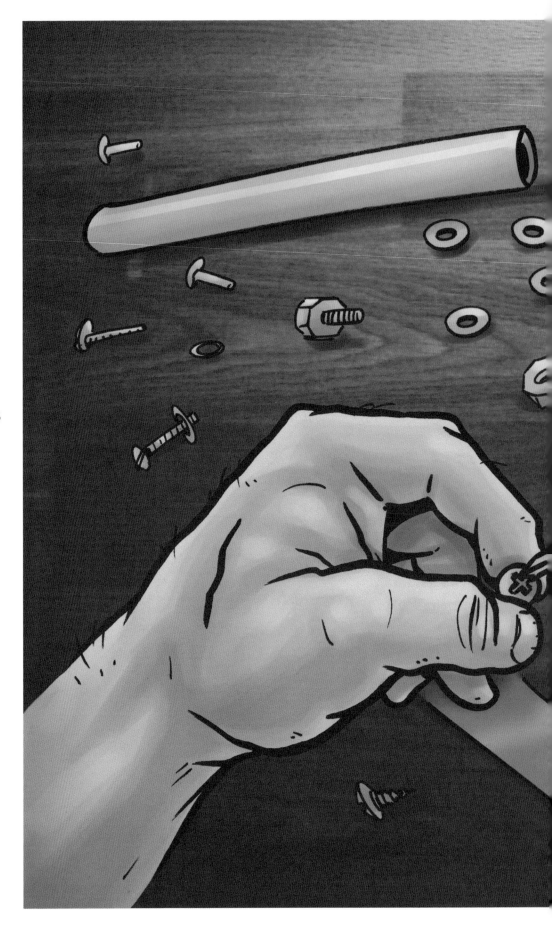

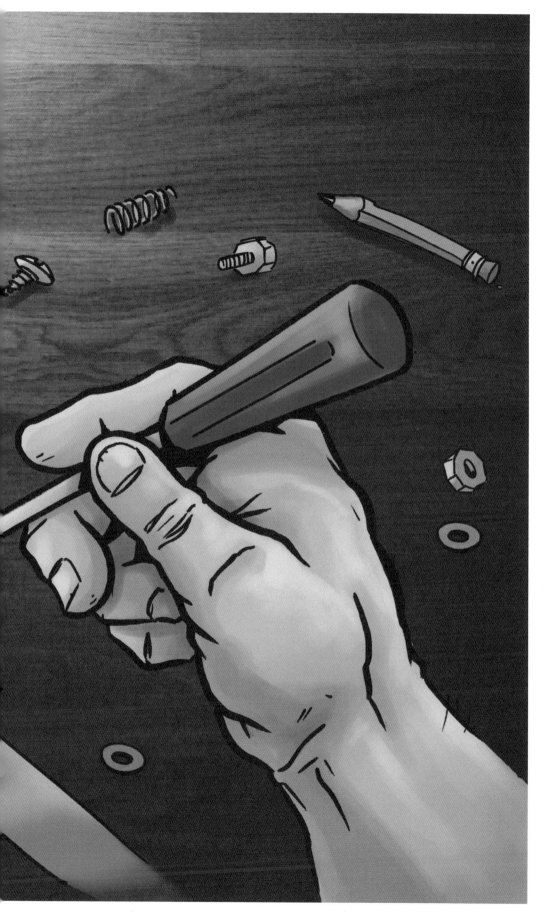

As his maker's hands moved across the rods, attaching them carefully together with each nut and bolt, he imagined his maker

making a fast

RACE CAR

that would zoom around a racetrack and take the checkered flag at the end of a race.

He imagined being made into a high flying **AIRPLANE** that would fly important people to far-away and exciting places.

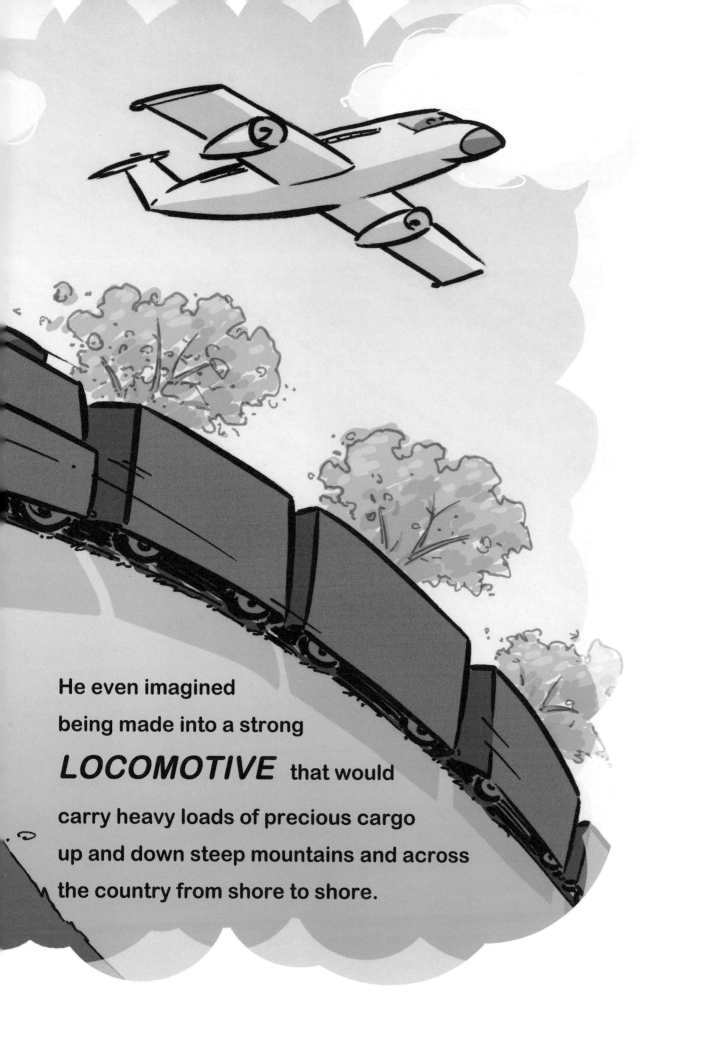

He even imagined
being made into a strong

LOCOMOTIVE that would

carry heavy loads of precious cargo
up and down steep mountains and across
the country from shore to shore.

But the thing he remembered most is his maker exclaiming,

"PERFECT!"

as he tightened the last bolt in place
and attached the wheels.

The maker smiled at his creation and said,
"That is it. I am finished.
I have created a wonderful child's wheelchair
for someone special to use."

"I am a
what?"
he thought.
"A child's

WHEELCHAIR?

How exciting is that?"
he continued to question in his mind.

Suddenly his mind was brought back to his surroundings by the ringing of the bell over the front door.

Someone had entered Matthews' Medicine Shoppe. But this was not the ordinary customer just coming in to get their prescription filled.

This was a stranger.

And he was carrying a little boy.

The wheelchair wondered to himself why the man was carrying the little boy; he was obviously big enough to walk.

He listened intently as Mr. Matthews greeted the stranger and they began to talk.

The stranger told Mr. Matthews that he was new in town and that his little boy, Timmy, had been unable to walk since birth.

Now that he was three, he was outgrowing the stroller they had been pushing him in and he was getting a little too big to carry everywhere.

The stranger went on to say that a neighbor had been so kind to tell him about Mr. Matthews' Medicine Shoppe and the neighbor even thought that he remembered seeing a *child's wheelchair* in the window.

As they walked slowly over to the window,
his heart began to race.

"Could this be the day someone takes me home?"
he thought.

Mr. Matthews eased him out of the window and dusted
off his seat. The stranger gently sat Timmy in his soft seat.

Timmy's hands timidly eased toward the wheels as he awkwardly pushed the chair for the first time.

Mr. Matthews and the stranger continued to talk as Timmy pushed his wheelchair up and down the aisles of the medicine shop.

The *faster* they went, the *happier* he was.

"What do
you think,
Timmy?"
Mr. Matthews
asked.

"This is *great!* " Timmy exclaimed with a smile.

"Now I don't have to have someone carry or push me
everywhere I go," he said excitedly.

For the first time since he was made,

the wheelchair knew what he was created to do.

He was filled with pride

at the thought of taking Timmy places

he had never been able to go before.

"Can I have it please, Dad?"
Timmy asked.
His face was still beaming
with a smile from
ear to ear.

"Let me see what
Mr. Matthews
and I can
work out,"
Dad said
to Timmy.

As his dad and Mr. Matthews continued to talk,
Timmy continued to push the chair anxiously up and
down the aisles.

As he waited impatiently on his dad,

Timmy quietly said to the wheelchair,

"If I get to take you home,

I am going to name you *Wally*.

We will do all the things

I have always wanted to do and never could."

As Mr. Matthews

and Timmy's dad

finished the purchase,

the wheelchair

thought to himself

humbly,

"I may have a name.

I may be

Wally the

Wheelchair."

He thought
how foolish he was
to want to be
a race car,
an airplane,
or a locomotive.

He could think of
no greater honor
than to be the one
to take Timmy
all the places
he had never
gone before.

"Come on, Timmy. The wheelchair is yours,"
his dad said cheerfully.

Timmy rolled the wheelchair
over to Mr. Matthews
and wrapped his
arms tightly
around his legs.

"Thank you," he said brightly.
"Thank you very much
for having this wheelchair
just for me."

"You are
welcome,
Timmy,"
he said
with a smile.

"I am going to name him Wally,"

Timmy proclaimed.

"He will be the one to take me all the places

I have always wanted to go,"

he continued.

"I think that is a great name for a wheelchair,"

Mr. Matthews replied to Timmy

as his eyes filled with tears.

"Come on, Timmy! Come on, Wally!"

Timmy's dad called as he opened the door.

Mr. Matthews watched as they left the shop

and rolled down the street.

He could not help but notice how proudly

Timmy rolled Wally down the street,

and just how brightly
Wally shined as Timmy rode
swiftly away.

The End.

44306460R00019

Made in the USA
Charleston, SC
20 July 2015